Udeh
Udeh, Onyinye
Love without flower

Author: Onyinye Udeh

Love without Flower

This book is a work of fiction. The names, characters, places, and incidents are products of the writer's imagination or have been used fictitiously are not to be constructed as real. Any resemblance to persons, living or dead, actual events, locals or organizations are entirely coincidental.

Edited by Ken @ www.FirstEditing.com
Cover art by Fran krailo @ www.krailoprinting.com

No part of this book may be reproduced or transmitted in any form or by any means electronic or mechanical including photocopying, recording or any information storage and retrieval system without prior written permission of the author.

    Copyright © 2015 Onyinye Udeh
      All Rights Reserved

Onyinye Udeh

Dedicated to God Almighty, the giver of Inspiration.

Love without Flower

Acknowledgments

To my parents; Mr. and Mrs. Ogbonna for being a pillar of support, showing me the path to love and teaching me all I know about life as it is today.

Ekeoma, Otuto, Chisom and Ugochukwu Ogbonna, Ngozi Onwo and Lovina Nwobodo (Mrs.) - my precious siblings; Thank you for your love, prayers and moral support, I couldn't have asked for better siblings than you all.

Mrs. Ifeyinwa Nwagbologu – my bosom friend and her beautiful daughter; Ogochukwu Nwagbologu for all their love and support towards my family ever since we met them here in the United States of America. Ogochukwu has been the big sister for my kids.

Mrs. Victoria Quashie – for her spiritual support and prayers for me and my family.

Miss Chidimma Umeizudike – for her support and selflessness in making my cover page beautiful.

My beautiful Children – Greatness and Amarachi Udeh, words cannot express how much I love you both. They are my source of joy and happiness and they inspired me in so many ways. They are the reason I sleep at night with a smile on my face and the reason I wake up with gratitude to God.

To the love of my life, – Edwin Udeh, thank you for being a driving force, a life coach, and my biggest fan. This book would not be a reality without you. I love you so much.

Onyinye Udeh

1

They are people of class, very wealthy and influential. The house, she found herself in, was a mansion, rich and luxurious fits its description. The floors were all slippery like glass. In all her life, she had never seen such luxury. There were hired servants, all properly and neatly dressed in uniforms, just as what one sees in a rich Western world; so when her mother-in-law opened the door to her bedroom for her, she was scared, although she managed to tip-toe in with a thought rushing through her head, *"is she pulling my leg?* Once in a while she opens her mouth and closes it in awe without making any sound. The room she found herself looked princess like; one can see that the bed was imported. The sheets were all satin, and the curtains looked lovely. The entire room smelt of luxury, she could not believe what her eyes were seeing. *Hope this is not one of my dreams*, she thought. "No, this is real," she said as she gently pinched herself, "this is real, I have left my poverty-stricken village to be in this heaven on earth?!" She did not know what to say or think. Then she suddenly remembered how she came there.

She smiled as she remembered home, Apata her village. It was a small village hidden right inside a valley surrounded by gigantic hills and huge trees. Most of the town's inhabitants have lived since the time of her forefather's, beautiful rich vegetation, palm trees, streams, and waterfalls, located in a sub-Saharan Africa. It was made up of several scattered huts, with fewer than 40 families. They, know each other by name and share their joy and sorrows together. That has been her home since her birth; a place where her umbilical cord was buried. She never left the village or dreamed of leaving at any point in her life. She has lived and seen people come and go, big, small, old and young; some were her age. Instead of getting tired or becoming weary, of how hard life can sometimes be, it has only made her fall in love more and more with Apata.

As a young girl of about 18 years old, growing up with her mother and with no man in the house, has not been easy. The physical and psychological toll, it had on both of them, cannot be hidden. Often has she imagined what life could have been with their father around? For all she can remember, she hardly knew who he was. According to her mother, he had suddenly taken ill one afternoon, after returning from the farm; they had done all that was within their power to save him, but it was all over before evening. For years now, they have learnt to live life the way they see it, but that does not mean that they were ready to give up. They had hope, and so each day that passes brought new hope, hoping for a better tomorrow, a tomorrow, that she had several times, doubted whether or not it would still come. On several occasions, she had woken in the middle of the night and found her mother crying; only God knows how she was able to make it so far without breaking down.

She will never forget the year they nearly lost their lives from food poisoning. How can she forget when she has a constant reminder, the two graves lying opposite each other in Mr. Akuma's compound, mother, and son? It could have been them; she is yet to know why they survived it, why God decided to spare their lives. That particular year was one of the most horrible years they ever had. It was the rainy season, the planting was going on, and almost everything had been sown to the ground, not nearing the time for harvest. That day she remembered they have gone to clean the church with few of their friends, and on coming back, they decided to pick some mushroom from a big, fallen tree. They were happy that finally they would have something to make their soup. It was the best they can afford, since they didn't have money for fish. That was how the other family met their death. They all ate their individual food and became sick. Unfortunately, they had picked the wrong mushrooms. The symptoms of food poisoning were there: diarrhea, vomiting; the villagers responded quickly to their call for help. They did all they could, to neutralize the poison with herbs and prayers. They survived it, but Mrs. Ojiugo and her son Okeh died within two days. He was supposed to be her age. So anytime she passes by their compound she trembles with fear that it could have been either her or her mother or both. Having lost her father at an early age, she was left with her poor mother. Their only source of income was the money they got by selling part of their farm produce. Many times, it was hard to have enough for themselves after selling their produce. She has learnt through the lengthy period of hardship, how to manage and be grateful without complaining. Such conditions could have cost her life; rather, it has refined her because she later grew up a beautiful, strong woman. Now when she looked back at those tough days, she wondered how it was possible for them to be where they are now.

Oluchi Muoka, for that was her name, was determined to make her mother happy one day. She never failed to encourage her whenever she saw that she was down and life kept going. It seemed as if God had not been hearing their cries as the years passed by, not until one day, one beautiful Christmas morning. The harmattan wind was at its peak and has taken its toll on everything. The trees have all shed their leaves and the forest was left bare. Everyone was freezing with cold, dried mouths, cracked feet, and the dust that seemed to rise at any little breeze.

Earlier that morning she had followed her friends to the stream to fetch a pot of cool, clean, drinking water; you have to get there early or else the stream would be dirty by other early risers, and to get a clean water will be difficult. But before that time, she had remembered waking up early, and shivering with cold, though she had covered herself with one of her mother's wrapper, but it didn't seem to have helped. It was still very early, so she had sat on her bed right beside her contemplating on whether she would be able to follow other girls to the stream when she heard them call her name. She hastily said her prayers and ran out from the room to fetch her water pot. She was just in time to catch up with them before they could pass her father's compound.

So as the manner of girls were while coming back they were giggling with excitement about the Christmas celebration; they talked about the gifts they had received, their new clothes and all the Christmas treats their family had for them. But the only one, who didn't say anything, was Oluchi. She listened quietly and smiled, trying hard to suppress her tears; and so when one of the girls suddenly asked her what she has gotten for the Christmas, she was startled because her mind was somewhere else. Spreading her palms, she bluntly answered, "I do not know… God will provide." And, suddenly they realized that all hands are not equal, one of them has been hurting, so one of the girls quickly changed the topic. Not very long, each disappeared to the path leading to their home, but they did not forget to invite their friend to be their guest.

Now Oluchi was by herself. As soon as she saw that they had gone far, she stopped and heaved a strong sigh of relief, placing her palms on her chest. Then she gently walked towards their compound. Immediately, when her feet touched their compound, she called on her mother, barely keeping her water from spilling.

"Mama, mama," Oluchi cried out.

"My daughter," Amoge answered, looking back as she tries to spread some vegetables in the sun.

"Oluchi, what is it?" she said, but this time leaving whatever she was doing and drawing closer to where her daughter was standing. She searched her face at the same time, and she could see that she looked worried. *She is always a happy type,* she thought, even after all of their sufferings, she had never for one day stopped laughing. Whatever it might be must be very serious.

When she was closer to her daughter, she looked closely to her face, lifting her face gently with her two hands, and then she told her to smile, "Smile my daughter, whatever it might be, make your mother happy.

Oluchi gently smiled, trying to suppress her tears.

"Now you have come my princess," her mother said, smiling.

"Yes mama, I am your princess, but did you know that we've not bought even a finger fish for this Christmas," Oluchi childishly said.

"My daughter," Amoge exclaimed, gently laughing. "Is that the problem?"

"Is it not enough mama," Oluchi nearly snapped. "See all my friends, they have all bought both their food and clothes; and look at us, unable to buy even the food to eat, and you are saying 'Is that all.'"

Then her mother couldn't stand it anymore; she wouldn't let her continue, so she quickly closed her mouth with her palm, "Don't talk again, my daughter," she pleaded, "You have said enough!"

She took hold of her hand and led her towards their door, making her sit on a low stool in front of their hut.

"I know all this my child," she softly said, looking directly at her face. When she saw that she has relaxed, she continued. "I was planning on coming and discussing things with you before you came up with it yourself; or do you think that I your mother does not care? Do you think that while other children will be celebrating with their new clothes that I would be sitting here unable to provide for my only child and feeling happy about it? No honey, your mother cares. I know that it is my responsibility to take care of…"

At that point, her countenance gradually changes as she poured her heart out to her daughter. And so, when Oluchi saw that she her mother was about to grieve, she quickly intervened, "No mama, I didn't mean to make you sad; it's OK mama," came her shaky voice. "Stop, don't please, have I ever complained?"

"I know my child," replied her mother, "I know that life would have been miserable without a child like you...."

"OK, now wipe your eyes mama," Oluchi gently said, looking closely at her face. Amoge quickly did as her daughter said; she dreaded anything that would cause her more sorrow. So she grabbed the edge of her wrapper and did wipe her eyes as Oluchi tried to calm her down. So on finding her voice again, she said, "My daughter, our God is not asleep; he is ever faithful."

"Yes mama," came Oluchi's voice as her mother continued.

"You know that chairman," her mother asked.

"You mean Mr. Fredrick?" Oluchi replied.

"Yes, that's him," Amoge answered.

"What happened to him?" she quickly inquired, thinking that something has gone wrong.

"Nothing Oluchi, I was about to tell you that he will be sharing rice and other food items to the widows in the village."

"What!?" shouted Oluchi.

"Yes, my daughter, Again,"???

Yes! Again, answered her mother,

"Oh! God bless him, amen my child and my friend mama …. You know Mama James?"

"Mama James…" Oluchi tried to remember, "Yes okay, the one you sweep the church with?"

"Yes, my daughter, that's her, she promised to give me some ingredients for the stew, her son returned and packed things in a carton for her."

"Thank God, mama; everything is almost settled, except fish.

"Don't worry, I will know what to do about that," her mother said.

"I think I saved a little money so that should not be a bother…Mama, mama," she called on her mother as if she has not been listening to what she was saying. Don't worry mama, if things becomes worst, I will follow the boys and go fishing this evening."

"Thanks, my child, I know what you can do, but it has not come to that, so let's hope that price of things will come down this morning."

2

After their discussion, Amoge instructed her daughter to get the local rice they already had, and start cooking while she went to buy the remaining things they needed. So while her mother was gone, Oluchi decided to build her fire first before she could then sit and pick some stones from the rice. She sings as she gathers the firewood and when she was through with making her fire, she ran into the hut and brought out the rice in a tray. She then carefully sat in front of their house and started picking. But just as she bent over singing as she picked, she felt someone's shadow leaning over her. She noticed that she was no longer alone; so she quickly raised her face to see who it might be, when she came face-to-face with a man. She was startled, it was a face she had never seen before, a total stranger; so she quickly rose up from where she sat, and drew back, but all this while the elderly man was looking at her, smiling.   Looking at him, Oluchi can see that he is rich. She tried to say something, but no words came. She was overwhelmed but just as she struggled with thoughts on who he might be, the man spoke first.

"No, my daughter," he said half smiling, "I've not come to scare you."

"Sorry sir, but are you looking for somebody?" Oluchi asked.

"Yes, my dear, am looking for somebody," he replied.

"Then who is it sir, let me see if I can be of any help to you." The word was still in her mouth, when something caught her attention; right in front of their house, cars had pulled up, expensive cars. She gasps in surprise as she asked "are all these people with you?"

He looked back, smiled and continued, "Yes, we've come for you."

Her eyes rolled in fear, "For me?" she screamed, holding her chest almost running.

"No dear," the man spoke again, "you don't have to fear, we have come for good."

Oluchi was still standing there perplexed when the men with him started off-loading things in front of their house, costly boxes as she could see *probably full of clothes* she thought, *bags of rice, cartons of food items.* She was almost in a shock when she repeated herself again, even when the man has already told her that they were here for her. "Sir, please, can you tell me who you people are and who you are looking for, because I don't think you are at the right place…Can somebody tell me what this is all about?"

She had started trembling with anxiety when her mother returned; at first, when Amoge saw the people gathering in her compound, people she never expected, her heart jumped. She thought that they were policemen. "Has anything happened to her daughter while she was gone? Gently carrying her little polythene bag with few things she had managed to buy, she gradually drew closer, looking at their faces; there she could see smiles on their faces as she passed that was when her heartbeats started coming down. When she got closer to where her daughter was standing and was able to see all kinds of things packed in front of her house, bags of food, boxes, she couldn't hold her surprise. The little bag she had gently held slipped from her hand, exposing the little fish she has purchased. Really, she was stunned. However, when she recovered from her shock though still gasping with surprise, she realized that it was time to find out who they were, but the elderly man just calmly smiled; he asked her if she will not offer them a seat and so she quickly told her daughter, who was standing by her side all the time, to help her as she ran to find seat. So when everyone was comfortably settled, then the elderly man softly spoke. He introduced himself as Sir Alex Desmond, and the woman with him, was his wife. "The people with us are members of my household and my friends. We have come to seek your daughter's hand in marriage."

The word marriage hit Amoge like a stone; she nearly screamed, "marr….what my dear, marriage?" After a moment, she screamed as tears poured down her face. "Are you sure you know who you are looking for?" She asked while observing their faces. "How do you know my daughter?

Sir Alex interrupted her, "Yes, we know," he politely said, "your daughter."   Goodness, Lord," she screamed and they all beamed with smiles at her outburst; but on seeing the neighbors gather, she was quietly told to try and control herself because the man with them is an influential man and would not like any gathering.

"Okay, if you say so, I will get a hold of myself." But then she sobbed and her daughter consoled her, tears pouring down her beautiful face, too. When the visitors finally revealed what the purpose of their coming was, she hastily excused herself, having instructed her daughter to hurry and prepare some food. She left and hurriedly went to her husband's brother, informing him that they had visitors. Not long after she returned, he followed suit, and he met them at the table. Oluchi and her mother had quickly prepared some food with the help of other family members. Mr. Julius Muoka happily welcomed them and was about to sit down when he suddenly noticed the presence of someone he knew. So it happened that they are not totally strangers; one of the men with him is a man from their community. Knowing that made both Oluchi and her mother very happy, by knowing that someone they can call their own is there, it brought much peace to their hearts. And the question of being strangers was gone. When Mr. Julius was told the purpose of their coming after the visitors had done with eating, he took it with joy. And as their plan was, they had wanted to leave with Oluchi the same day. The father of the groom, who was abroad, had persisted that he was willing to do all necessary marriage rites that same day; however, Mr. Julius had refused. He told them to come back in a month's time because he has to make some inquiries himself. My people say, "One should not be in a haste to answer the call of a deity, lest he dies by the deity." That is how the journey of marriage is; you take your time and do things the way it should be done. Yes, they came with one of their kinsmen, but he is not yet satisfied; moreover, he has to inform all of his kinsmen that somebody is seeking their daughter's hand in marriage. According to him, Oluchi is not only his; she is the daughter of all."

So they all agreed and he happily stayed until when the visitors finally left. The guest had left, but the house of late Mr. Ignatius Muoka later turned out to be the center of the celebration that day. As soon as they turned their backs, an instruction was given by Mr. Julius to pass a message to the entire village. They are to assemble in his father's compound because something great has happened. Someone has come to ask their daughter's hand in marriage. That was how it was known, so as the message was being sent, there was a big preparation going on, as different delicacies and drinks were being provided. Not only did their visitors come with bags of food item, but as they were leaving Sir Alex had given them a huge amount of money, so they were prepared to feed the people. What seemed to be the toughest season of their lives had turned to be the best of all! Oluchi could not control her tears as she watched people, her friends eat in their house, and in her excitement, she decided to open the boxes brought by their visitors. They were filled with clothes some her size and those that did not fit, which she gave out to her friends.

When Oluchi's father had died, they were left with the only close the relations they had with Mr. Julius Muoka. He was a farmer with several mouths to feed so it has not been easy for him, but he had always been doing his best. He was always there to support them both financially and otherwise, and so he gained their respect and trust. So in this particular issue, he took it upon himself to do as he had promised. Next month seems far, but before one will know it, it will come around; so whatever he has to do, he will do it quickly. Actually, the only source of information, he has about Sir Alex and his family, is Theophilus. So his source of information is limited because Sir Alex is from a different state entirely; so one particular morning, he decided to pay Theophilus a visit. He purposely went earlier than expected because he would not like to risk missing him. He wanted to take him by surprise.

Onyinye Udeh

To Oluchi life had automatically changed, now she has a different thought; she looked more beautiful than before. She was happy that all their stress and sorrows were all over. No more rising up early for farm work or scraping the bottom of their pot to get enough food. Now they have more than enough, enough to give to their friends as they come to rejoice with them. So while her uncle was busy trying to gather some information about their in-laws to be, Oluchi was busy too in her mind, thinking on what it means to be a married woman. The whole thing had come as a surprise to her, she has never dreamed that whenever she will marry, it will be in such haste or to someone that she has never met or even seen. So the one month of waiting was to her own advantage, because while she waited for the month to come by, she started living in a dream world. Oluchi started imagining what life will be living with a man to call her husband; the word husband always gave her goose pimples. She started thinking on what her fiancé would look like, is he tall or short? *Oh! He better be tall like his father* she would think to herself. What type of man is he, is he capable of loving, a kind and patient man, someone that will be able to look through her and see who she really is? After all, that has been her dream. Oluchi suddenly realized as she looked at the diamond ring on her finger that her status as a single woman would soon change to that of a married woman. She began to build a strong attachment to their family; she could no longer wait to set eyes on him. She didn't know how possible it could be, but she has realized that she was already in love. *Is it possible* she will ask herself? *Is it possible to fall in love with someone you've not seen or known?* Whether it is possible or not, she was already in love. In one of her daydreams, she had spoken up without knowing that her mother was close enough to hear her; she had dreamed on how her first kiss will be, "Awkward, I guess," she had answered herself.

"What is awkward, my daughter, I hope you're not sick for being so excited," her mother said, coming closer and feeling her forehead with her palm. "Thank God, it's not hot!" Oluchi smiled calmly.

Although she wanted to be married, Oluchi nearly refused to go with her mother-in-law to be when they finally came to take her with them. Suddenly, she realized everything was becoming real so she was moved to tears. Oluchi sobbed with bitterness as if something terrible had happened; it was so much that her mother and uncle had to take her inside their room to talk to her. Her mother wept, too, as she covered her daughter in a warm embrace.

"It is difficult my daughter," she said. "My daughter, it's okay to cry; we understand, but you shouldn't cry as if something terrible has happened. Just see how much you have brought to this family, aren't you happy? Your husband is in abroad and very soon he will come and take you."

"OK mama," she said in her broken voice, "it's just that they are total strangers; we know my daughter, and that was why your uncle refused until he was able to make some inquiries." Oluchi nodded in affirmation to all that her mother had said, but then her uncle stepped in.

"I am not surprised at your tears, dear, it is normal for any girl marrying to cry; wipe your tears mama, come …come to your uncle." She gently left her mother and embraced her uncle.

The very day the Alex family went to bring their bride home. Sir Alex did not go with them having agreed with his wife to organize a grand welcome party secretly for his daughter- in-law. He thought it will better if he stayed, seeing that there are so many things to be done. So it was his wife and some members of the family that went. So he had waited patiently for their arrival, calling as often as he can to be sure that all was going as planned. On the other hand, Oluchi, too, was anxious. She was putting her whole life in the hands of people she know nothing about, but as they traveled she began feeling more relaxed. She couldn't imagine herself sitting on an airplane. Who could have imagined that, it was all fun and before their flight could land, the driver was already waiting for them? *Wow!* She thought. She had for the first time traveled out of her village; oh yes, life was sure good. So, on arriving home that evening, Oluchi could not believe her eyes when the door of the car was opened for her as she stepped out. In front of her was a large compound, the house was a mansion; there were so many thoughts in her mind as she looked at her mother-in-law, who was standing close to her; she could almost read her mind before she gently said, "Welcome home dear, from now onwards, this is your home."

She has never imagined that in one point in her life she will find herself in a beautiful place as what she is seeing; she could hardly control her nervousness, as they attended to her like a princess. The reception, they gave her, was a special one, so she didn't expect it as her eyes swelled with tears. They all stood quietly smiling at her reaction, "Yes, my dear, come with me." Her mother- in-law's voice startled her. "Remember, there are people waiting to welcome you." When they entered the house, again she was not in a haste to see anyone; she took her time to admire what she saw, and they were glad to explain to her about some of the pictures that had captured her eyes. That was when she finally agreed that things had changed for her.

She was taken to her room by Mrs. Desmond as they were taking her luggage away. As they approached the door leading to her room, Mrs. Desmond slowly opened it for her, ushering her in with smiles. "Once more, welcome home, this is your room." Oluchi quietly stepped in looking so amazed of how beautiful everything looked; she could see that the room was very large. She looked at her beautiful bed and its sheets, satins that is what they were she said within her as she feels them, and hastily moved to look through the window to see the view. There she felt nature whisper to her, as the cold evening breeze swept across her face. Everything looked gorgeous; her eyes sparkled with life as she calmly turned, looking steadily to the woman who was standing close to the door. She quickly ran into her arms in tears. "Thank you, auntie," she softly said, "it is beautiful!"

"I am happy you love it dear. I should be the one thanking you; it's nothing," Mrs. Desmond said almost in a whisper, smiling. "Now you have to hurry. Remember, you've not seen your father-in-law."

When she said that, Oluchi was startled. "Oh yes," came her voice. "What a fool I've been!"

"It's OK. Take your time, now here are your clothes for the party," Mrs. Alex said, gently picking a lovely evening gown from the bed.

"For me!" Oluchi exclaimed with excitement.

"Yes dear, for you," said Mrs. Desmond.

"Thanks, mama, I love it," said Oluchi.

"Now I will be leaving you. I will be coming around to see how you are doing, just before you come down to see our friends," Mrs. Desmond said.

Oluchi, full of smiles and still holding her clothes against her body, gently nodded. When Mrs. Desmond left the room, Oluchi was happy; now she had gone, she said to herself, *let me take my time and look at things properly.* Then she quickly grabbed her beautiful gown, measured it to herself and laughed, raising her hand in appreciation to God, "how I wish my mother were here to see for herself, but don't worry mama," she quietly said, "very soon, you will come for child visit, in my house, OK?"

When Mrs. Desmond left Oluchi and walked directly to the maid's quarters to see how the party preparation was going. Upon reaching the quarters, she assigned a maid to Oluchi, giving her instructions to see that young Alex's wife was taken good care of before she comes down. After seeing that all was in order, she now hurried to her bedroom. There she met her husband walking up and down; he was tired of waiting. "How did it go dear," he hurriedly said immediately she entered the room. She gently approached him, giving him a kiss on the cheek, "Relax dear, it all went as you wished, but right now she is overwhelmed."

"Oh yes, right now," Sir Alex muttered. He then turned away from his wife. One should have expected him to be happy; but rather, it seems as if he was not pleased. He suddenly looked like someone in pain, someone anxious about something, as you look into his eyes you can see the fear. "When do I see her?" he asked.

"I will let you know when she is ready," the wife said as she leaves the room. The party was to be held at night, but before it was evening the house was already full. The host, on the other hand, had taken the time to see that all was going as they planned. There was plenty to eat and drink. There was no fear of running out of things since all arrangements were carried out by a well-known hotel. But just as the party was in its full swing, suddenly there was a hush as silence swept the through the whole room.

"See who we have here, friends," said Mrs. Desmond. All the guests' attention went to where she standing. There they saw someone gracefully coming down the stairs, and she was a beauty; the guests smiled and looked at each other's faces. And now the noise has once more started as they all inquired as to who she was. Oluchi was looking gorgeous. All traces of poverty had disappeared; no one would have doubted it if she were said to be a princess. She looked nervous, but the father-in-law, who was standing just beside her, said. "Easy child, remember you are my daughter now."

So as she was led down the stairs, a round of applause was heard as Sir Desmond happily introduced her to his friends. They all went wild with excitement as some came to make acquaintance with her. As Oluchi stood and received greetings from the people, she noticed that as people came and went, their expressions changed. She was quick enough to see a lady shaking her head as if she were pitying her, but she could not understand why. By this time, she was about getting a bit worried at those looks. That's when a young, handsome man slowly approached them smiling; he gently bowed as he addressed Mrs. Desmond.

"Please excuse me. I'd like to introduce myself to your daughter-in-law Auntie Margaret."

"Oh! Go ahead Charles," Mrs. Desmond responded. Then Charles gently took Oluchi's hand, trying to lead her away. Oluchi was reluctant, but then Mrs. Desmond quickly intervened, saying, "Go ahead dear, and remember this is your night."

So though being very shy, she agreed to dance with Charles. Oluchi later learnt as they danced that Charles is Bar. Wilson's son, Bar. "Wilson is an old friend of the family, your family is my family," Charles had explained. "I was standing with my mother when I saw you come down; you see I couldn't resist coming to you, even if your husband were here, I would have done the same."

As soon as he mentioned Oluchi's husband, her eyes sparkled. Actually she hadn't heard much about him and would be glad if she can get something from Charles. So she quickly jumped at the opportunity.

"So you know him," she said smiling.

"Oh yes… but not for a long time," he replied. "As we grew up, we separated." He struggled to say, becoming uncomfortable.

Oh! Yes, I know, Oluchi again answered to herself.

"He traveled overseas at a very young age. I am glad you know," said Charles. He was relieved as he hurriedly changed the topic. The party was a success as planned, but it was full of mixed feelings. It was obvious that all is not well come to think of it. What in the world could have made Sir Alex's younger son miss his father's party when it was clear that he did not travel? So while Oluchi was in her room, her mind ran through all that she was able to notice as she stood undressing herself with the help of her maid. And for now she had a maid who would take care of her.

"Martha," she gently called on her maid, "I am so excited."

"I can see, madam," Martha gently said, smiling too.

"Martha," she called again, and stopping what they were doing. "I want you to tell me something about my husband, anything, anything you know about him. Is he handsome? Is he kind, madam?"

Martha interrupted her, "I am sorry, I know little about him."

"Why, little Martha, when you have lived here for years."

"I know madam, but I am only a maid. I only come when he calls for me, anytime he is around."

"Now I understand," Oluchi gently said, smiling. "Don't worry Martha, when he comes back, you will always see him as you come to attend to me.

Just then, as they were deep in their conversation, they were startled by a noise. Oluchi was baffled, but Martha was busy and acted as if she hadn't heard anything. The noise sounded like an argument.

"Don't worry madam, it's Sam… Sir Alex's son," Martha said.

"Did he have another son," Oluchi asked in surprise.

"Yes madam, but where was he all this while? That is Master Samuel for you, his life, you cannot tell, always quarreling with the father."

"I see," replied Oluchi. "That is what you see with father and son in most families. It is no problem. I will be glad to meet my husband's brother." And as she said that, she hastily hurried her dressing and stepped outside amidst

Martha's call not to go. She hurried in the direction of the noise. Just as she was out, down the long corridor and about to turn, she came face-to-face with father and son. "Papa," she said smiling.

"My daughter," Sir Alex gently answered; he looked angry but on seeing Oluchi he tried to put on a smile. Then Oluchi turned her gaze to Samuel, who was standing just opposite her. "Please introduce me to your son, papa," she said smiling. "No!" said the elderly man's voice. "I will not, now go back to your room!"

"Please papa," Oluchi said, "Whatever it may be, remember this is my night, no papa, no room for anger," she playfully said, and then extended her hand to Sam.

"I am your brother's wife. I am glad to meet you," she said.

Samuel was moved by her lovely nature, he could not but gladly answer, "You are kind,"

"Papa, it's okay," Oluchi said as she again turned to her father-in-law. "I hope my husband is as handsome as he is." Once she said that, she quickly noticed how the two men had reacted, for Samuel quickly withdrew his hand from hers and walked away hastily, and Sir Alex turned his face away in pity, but he soon regained himself as he led her to her room. She later learnt that he was angry with him for not being present at her welcome party.

3

As he walked down the stairs away from the court premises, the press thronged him. He has just won a case he had against the federal government. It is very interesting to see a man fight the government single-handedly and win. He must be an extraordinary fellow. The only thing that seemed to have made him extraordinary was his wealth, powerful in all his ways, influential, and an engineer by profession. He is into the oil business, construction, and the case, he had with the government, was about the oil found in his land. But notwithstanding, despite all of these things his joy has never been full. That had been the life of Sir Alex Desmond.

Actually, he had a son who was believed to live abroad, but it is only people that knew him so well, knew that his son has not stepped out from his room after his eighth birthday. When he shared with his family his plan to get a wife for his son, they were greatly against it, His wife and his younger son had tried to reason with him, but he rather took offence; he refused their advice. "I am disappointed," he had yelled, "if only his mother were alive… do we not marry for our beloved dead one, just to preserve the lineage. Why not my son? What is wrong in marrying for him?"

Then, on seeing his outburst, they kept quiet and watched him. Anyone, who knows him, knew it would not be advisable to say a word at that moment, but when he was done speaking, his wife gently told him that it not a good decision. "Young Alex is very ill," she said, "Try to understand, we love him, the same as you do. Yes, we marry for our dead ones, but the tradition is slowly fading away. What about the young girl who is involved? Have you considered telling her family that your son is sick?"

He had listened very quietly, but that did not solve any problems. And even when his younger son tried to persuade him to drop the idea, he refused; he became more furious than before and so the meeting ended in disagreement. It didn't come as a surprise to the family. The wife knew that when it comes to issues concerning Alex junior, his word is always final. Most often, she had become so frustrated knowing that the thought of junior had taken every part of his being. He neither had time for her or her son. They have tried their best to make him see things correctly, but it has yielded nothing. And now they have no option other than to accept things the way they are. She had agreed to marry him for the wrong reason; it was his money that she was after, but now she can see how wrong she was. They both need his love, too. She was forced to change her opinion as she watched herself and her son beg to be part of his life. The money was there, but there was no happiness. , junior is all that he knew. So after that night she decided to give him her support, but Samuel stood his ground; he would never be part of it. Because according to him, 'it is against his conscience."

That night, when the meeting ended the way it did, Samuel was not happy; the rest of the night, as he walked out from the room feeling rejected and unaccepted, he believed that he had reached a certain age that his father would try to reason with him. But instead, he trashed his suggestions as if they were nothing. So as he lay on his bed, he came to conclusion that all, that happened, was as a result of him not being his biological son; he narrowed it down to the time when he was just a little boy. There was an incident that made him realize that although he calls him father, he could not pretend to have loved him with the same measure of love he had for junior.

That very day, he has gone to play with the only brother he had. Junior was a little older than him, so he sees him as his elder brother. At that time, his illness had started, but it has not taken its toll as it later did. He could play a little with him, so in the course of their play he playfully snatched his toy from him. He was teasing him to come and get it back, knowing full well that he could not get up from the wheelchair. Junior had pleaded and tried to grab it anytime he'd bring it closer to him. The teasing continued until junior fell off his wheelchair while he was trying to get back his toy; it was then that I realized how far I have gone as I screamed and called for help. Junior was sprawled on the floor trying to help himself, sobbing helplessly.

He will not forget how furious their father was as he came to his son's rescue; he nearly hit mother that day for not keeping closer eyes on them; and as for him shaking and sobbing, he furiously warned me never to hurt his son. Let it not repeat itself, he had yelled. I never understood all the word he had said, but his countenance said it all. That was that was how it has been; he had grown to love junior so much that he dreads ever making him cry. But in all of this Sir Alex's attitude towards him and his mother had remained the same. It was clear to them that the only one, that matters in his life, is junior. Sam also remembered his reaction the day he told him that he is about to be married; he would have liked to have his blessing before he announced his engagement. He will not forget the look on his father's face; his countenance had suddenly changed as if he had committed a crime. He had bluntly refused and told him that it will not happen in his house. He told Samuel there is no way he could be married before junior. He said that he is his elder brother, and he had to respect that. "Tradition said so and even if our tradition would allow it, I will not live to see you marry before my son," Sir Alex said.

That was how their quarrel started; he had learnt to overlook so many wrongs from him, but in this particular issue he vowed to carry on with his plans, with or without his support. But his mother had intervened and told him to hold on with his plans until it was settled, and he had heeded her advice. Later on, when Sir Alex came up with the issue of marrying for junior, he had told him to count him out if he will not listen to any advice. All he had wanted, since he was a boy, is a father like every other child, but it didn't happen; he couldn't do anything that would please him. The way, he acts and treats him seriously, indicates that he would prefer him to be sick, rather than junior. He had tried to love him as his father, but he had indirectly been refused through his father's attitudes. Often, he had wished that he was not a part of this family. He did not blame him for being unhappy about his son's condition, but time had passed enough to where he should accept it. He should accept that it was never his or any anyone else's doing.

Sir Alex had worked hard in his life to be what he had finally become. He has had little or no help from anyone. All his life he has refused to live an average life; he wanted something more. There was something in him that kept driving him, telling him he that he could reach wherever he wanted in life. But before that time, it was like all odds were against him, no money and no child. Eventually, when their prayers were answered, everything seemed to be coming together at the same time as the child. Doors were opening, but just as they were about to enjoy the fruit of their patience and ease themselves off stress, death came and snatched his wife from him. It took him years to recover from the shock, for he had wept uncontrollably; he was bitter that she did not live to enjoy life a little after their long years of struggling. He mourned her for years and, as a result, had a nervous breakdown.

As he lay closer to his present wife, who was not happy with the way things had gone that night after the party was over, he could see that she was not happy about the little quarrel he had with Samuel. He was full of thoughts about his son, "No one can take his place in my heart." He had gone ahead and married for him, but now he felt that he had made a mistake, and his conscience had suddenly begun to trouble him, but he was determined to suppress it. *It didn't come as a surprise,* he thought, *I have prepared for it before now, I will wait until the right time."*

4

The next morning brought the family together as they came to have their breakfast. Oluchi had never imagined that the next breakfast, she would have after leaving her village, would be with people she hardly knew, in a setting she had never dreamed of. Though before that time, she had woken up in a start as if she were escaping from a bad dream. She had looked by her side and couldn't find her mother and was beginning to be troubled when she remembered that she is now in a city. She had left her mama, Apata at her village. They were all that she knew. She wondered what her mama was doing right now.

Love without Flower

During those years of trial she had longed for a place of refuge, a place where she could be by herself and dream of all the good things anytime she was hurting. She found it in a lone, barely surviving cotton tree right there in her village closer to their house; it was the only cotton tree she had ever seen. She heard that cotton grows in Africa but thrives more in the Western world. Again, that the cotton wool, she sees, is gotten from the cotton tree; knowing that has added to the good feelings she had for the tree. She was a little girl at that time, 7 years old to be precise, so anytime she was hurting, hungry, she would go to the tree to play and see how it's been thriving. Anytime she has a little scratch, whether it is bleeding or not, she will go to the tree, pluck the cotton with a little saliva on it and treat herself to its healing powers. She so much wearied the tree with her constant plucking and coming that it later dried up and died.

That day she was hurting and decided to visit her tree and found it dry, she had cried as if she had lost a friend; she knew that she would always remember, that tree, as if it had been her friend. So as she was still thinking of home, looking around the huge beautiful room she found herself, she heard someone knock at the door; it was Martha. She had come to inform her that breakfast was ready. Then she had hurriedly dressed and rushed to the bathroom to freshen up before coming down to join her family. Oluchi was a little nervous as she joined them. They all expected it as they tried to engage her in a conversation; they wanted to know how she was getting used to her new home so far, how well her night was without her mother. It did work because she was able to relax and say a few words.

Sam never said much, actually this was his first time seeing how she really looked; so once in a while he stole a glance at her and pitied her so much. It was only pity that he felt for her. He could not imagine how poor the family must have been to have allowed their child to go with a man they never knew before; but then he was startled as Oluchi gently called him, "Sam, I would like you to tell me anything about your brother when we are through." "Do you mean junior?" Sam hastily said as the question had caught him unprepared.

"Yes, who else?" she asked.

"I will, okay, when I think we have enough time to get acquainted with each other. You are not leaving tomorrow?" Sam asked.

"Now finish your breakfast," Sir Alex intervened.

"I am sorry papa, I guess am being too outspoken," Oluchi pleaded.

"It's okay dear," Mrs. Alex said. "Just as Sam had said, we have plenty of time to discuss and answer all of your questions, okay."

Sam and his mother had suddenly lost their appetites as soon as Oluchi brought up the issue of young Alex; they had kept quiet as they watched their father's countenance change. He later stood up and excused himself, "I am running late to the office," he said as he leaves.

5

Before Oluchi had come to live with the Alex family, the arrangement was that her husband will be back in nine month time for their wedding; but for the time being, she had to be taught to bring her to the standards of the family. There are things that were expected of her as a wife to a prince. She has to be a lady, the way she talks and carries herself matters a lot. She did not argue it. She had quickly agreed to the plan, knowing that there is no way she can fit into the new environment she has found herself without being taught from scratch. She had been awkward in most of what she did and was glad to learn things their way. So she was being exposed to their lifestyle and before one could know it, she was transformed.

However, as time passed by Oluchi realized that she had more than she could ever imagine having, except that she was beginning to feel terribly lonely. She knew no one and so having a visitor was ruled out She could not socialize as she wanted to and anywhere she wants to go someone must go with her. *This is not what she had bargained for* she thought. She also discovered within the short time that she had spent there that life in that house was queer. She had been speaking with her husband and that had gone a long way to settle most of her fears, but he had not come back as planned; they kept postponing things, and that's when she realized that they put more emphasis on things that doesn't really matter to her and seem to forget what the original plan was: her wedding.

She had expected that on her arrival, all their focus will be on the wedding plan, but nobody ever says anything about wedding. There's been no shopping, no hiring of a hall, although Alex has promised to buy most of the things she would need, but that does not mean that there would be no other plans. The atmosphere had just remained the same. So at a point when she could no longer bear it, she decided to confide in someone; someone who would understand her and see things from her own point of view. She had come to agree that Sam has always been there for her; they all have been, but she knew that she did feel more comfortable talking with him. So she decided to look for Sam and finally met him at the bar. She was looking worried as she talked, so Sam, seeing how she looked, decided to take her away from the bar. He took her to a place where they could talk without people hearing them. He stood near her and intently stared at her. Sam was suddenly carried away by her looks, and he was moved to kiss her. Then Oluchi was startled as she tried to free herself. "No Sam… Stop it," she said. "Have you forgotten that I am your brother's wife?"

"Oluchi, listen to me," he said. He shook her this time as he tried to make her listen to what he has to say. "I am going to say it once and no more, I want you to leave this house, tomorrow!"

"What! What are you talking about? I can see you're drunk," Oluchi said and tried to free herself.

"I am not drunk. I am sober as the morning sun. I can help you if you are willing to leave," Sam said.

"You should be ashamed…" But before she could finish what she was saying, Sam had hurriedly left in anger and she was thrown into confusion. She quickly followed him, but she could not catch up with him. So she decided to go and see his mother instead. She met Auntie Margaret lying on her bed and hastened to her. And as Aunt Margaret tried to get up from the bed she could see that Oluchi looked troubled. "What is it dear, you looked disturbed."

"I am auntie, it's Sam. I don't understand what it was, but he just told me to leave this place."

"What place?" Mrs. Desmond had asked looking puzzled, "to go home, but why should he say that to you? Then it struck her, now she tried to cover up, "Maybe he has been drinking," she softly said watching her reaction.

"As if you know, he had been. Actually, I met him at the bar, now I see, he is not himself. He wanted to kiss me and I refused," Oluchi said.

"He did!" she almost shouted. "Why in heaven would he do that? I am ashamed, I am so sorry dear. I know he meant no harm.

"I thought so, too, I will see that he never tries it again."

"Now go to your room, there is nothing to worry about."

"Good night auntie."

"Sweet dreams, dear."

In Apata village, the news of Oluchi's marriage has spread like wildfire. For some weeks that followed, her mother had continued to entertain their numerous visitors. She never hesitated to tell their callers that she will be traveling to town for her daughter's wedding. But as months passed and nothing was heard from Oluchi, she became terrified. She was so much overwhelmed with fear that one evening she took her lantern and walked down to the brother-in-law's compound to tell him of her fears. She found him half asleep on the chair, so without wasting time she went straight to what she came for. But looking at how calm Mr. Julius looked, you would think that he was not touched by what he was hearing; but while Amoge was talking, he was really troubled; but he has managed to stay calm. Just like Amoge had realized that all is not well, he also was becoming worried because things had not turned out the way they expected. He wouldn't want to show how terrible he feels, so he had managed to respond very calmly as if nothing has happened.

"There is no cause for alarm, Amoge," he said. "Remember, I made time to see Theo myself; besides, our in-laws did not come on their own; it was one of us who brought them, so relax. I know who to run to when the time comes.

But for now let's give them another month and see what happens. Before then, I will go to his father and see what help we can get from him."

Actually, he had done as he promised but with no success, but according to Theo's father, he had traveled abroad and they have not heard from him. On hearing the news, Mr. Julius was furious with Theo's father, but seeing that there was nothing to be done he walked away from the compound in anger. When he got home, he called Amoge and told her that all is not well, and there is no way they can reach Theo.

She refused to believe it and screamed for help. The villagers gathered, and the women tried to calm her down. They told her that all hope was not lost, but she refused to be comforted. "I know that wherever she is right now she needs me," she cried out. She refused to be consoled and gradually she became sick after several efforts by the community to reach her daughter had failed. No one was to blame; they had thought that since it was their kinsmen that brought them their in-laws to their house that there was nothing to be afraid. They never expected it would turn out this way. It was a deal Theophilus, Mbanefo had with Sir Alex. Theo, has been pestering him to link him up with his connections and Alex had refused, until Theo brought up the issue of finding a beautiful maiden for his sick son.   So Theo was paid, and his papers to travel abroad were given to him in a couple of months. According to their agreement, the deal expired the day Oluchi came to town with them. He knew Alex so well and would not like to risk his anger. So he had traveled as soon as he could. Theo was the type his people would recommend for any political post if there were any opportunity for they trusted him. They trusted him so much, but what they didn't know about him was that he was ready to do anything for money.

That night, after Oluchi left her mother-in-law, she entered her room and sat on her bed. She began recalling all that had happened since she arrived. She came to agree that all has been going on well, *except that her husband had refused to come home* she thought, and anytime she tried to present the issue to her father-in-law, his only reply would always be, he would be back very soon. He always smiled whenever he said that, but she would not deny that she had never seen pity in those eyes. Apart from being exceptionally good to her, she had come to know him as a man who keeps to himself, except when drinking his wine.

Oftentimes, she had seen him enter a particular room on a regular basis, more than any of the other rooms. She would not forget what happened the time she came to live with them. A few weeks after her arrival, he had called her one evening and as she sat listening to what he had to say; he had told her not to enter a particular room, anyone else can, even the maids you may be seeing them enter but don't you do it.

"Why …papa," Oluchi had curiously asked. "Is there anything I should know that you've not told me?"

"Yes," he had answered quickly. Looking into the distance, he paused. "I think I will tell you, but at the right time."

To Oluchi, that was the beginning of her curiosity, the beginning of her troubles. Now she wanted to know, in her little mind. She felt that Sir Alex must be an occult man, "Oh no!" she gasps, "Is that why Sam told me to leave?" *No, Sam was drunk* she said to herself, *tomorrow, I will tell my friend.*

Next day she did not waste time to sharing her troubles with her friend, Martha. She had become her bosom friend apart from her people. On that day, she had called her in, to her room. Martha was busy with other house chores when she heard her call. She then hastily left what she was doing to answer her, thinking that maybe she will want her to run an errand; but as she knocked at the door and opened it, smiling as was her manner, she was surprised to see how terrible Oluchi looked. She knew that it is more than what she had thought, *madam is not happy* she said within her. She slowly shut the door behind her and gently walked towards where Oluchi was lying on the bed. Martha sat closely to her side, placing her hand on her back as she looked directly at her face asking her what the matter was, "You are disturbed madam?"

"I am Martha," Oluchi said sighing, "I don't know, but I feel that something is not right."

"You mean here, in this house?" Martha asked.

"Yes, can't you see? Aren't we supposed to be planning my wedding, shopping, but nothing is happening, we are now at eight months and my husband has yet to come back? No, something is wrong. I have to tell you because you know how it is with me. I hardly know anybody outside your people, hardly do things the way I feel. Can't you see that I am like a prisoner here," she almost yelled. "You have to help me; can you take me to your house?"

"Why? What do you think is wrong with this house?" Martha asked.

"I am scared of staying here take me to your house," Oluchi said.

"Which house?" Martha almost snapped. Please madam, I don't have anywhere to take you, we are poor; besides, I don't know what you are talking about… but madam…" She seemed to have lost what she wanted to say as she paused, and then she continued. "You can run away."

"Run away," Oluchi asked, "why should I run when nothing is wrong here? Does that mean you know something?"

"You said you want to leave," said Martha.

"Martha, where, where do I go from here?"

Oluchi had become hysterical, almost out of her mind. "I have nowhere to run to; I don't know my left from my right. I've barely stepped outside since I came here, maybe you will take me to your house, anywhere…."

"Good heavens," Martha interrupted. "Didn't I say I have no place?" Martha suddenly became alarmed, "No, no! We don't want Sir Alex trouble!"

"You look scared Martha," Oluchi said suspiciously, "Why?"

"I am scared madam," Martha replied.

"What do you know, Martha, tell me?"

"Why don't you leave me alone, I am only a servant," Martha said.

"Tell me what you know," Oluchi insisted. Now Martha was sobbing, she was afraid, of everything, afraid of her life, afraid of losing the only job she had known for years. But she had to do what she got to do and prayed for the best she told herself. Oluchi had been so kind to her that she will not let anything hurt her. She told her that she had lived in that house enough to know a little of everything; nothing is really wrong here, except that it has been often rumored that Sir Alex is an occult man, what! Oluchi was in horror, "Please madam, and get a hold of yourself. I guess you might have seen him enter a particular room. I think he may be hiding someone's body there." At that point, Oluchi screamed. "Please madam," Martha pleaded. "I am not sure it is true, but I have to tell you what I know, so don't scream. Somebody might hear us, and that will be more trouble, take this. This may calm your nerves," Martha suggested as she handed her a glass of wine; she had gone to get it when she saw how nervous Oluchi has become.

Later that day after her discussion with Martha, it was like her whole being was shut down. She had lost interest in everything and she couldn't think straight. So as she sat opposite the dresser looking at herself in the mirror, she remembered the discussion she had with Sam the previous night. And then she was startled as she thought, "Is *that why Sam told her to leave?* She could remember that he was very angry with her on meeting. He never said anything but his countenance said it all, *I must have been a fool,* she thought, *why didn't I see it?*

She regretted how she had acted. She made up her mind to go and plead with Sam to give her a second chance and to forgive her foolishness. She was ready to listen and do whatever he says, so before it was bedtime, she secretly went to Sam; he accepted her apology, but there was nothing more to say, and he had softly told her, "I have already risked my father's anger, if he ever finds out that I have attempted telling you anything, the outcome will not be a pleasant one. I am sorry. I hope you would understand me."

Sam had been trying very hard to avoid Oluchi since he noticed that he was attracted to her. When she first came all that he felt for her was pity; he had never imagined that he will fall for someone that has a different upbringing like she had. Now everything has changed as he watched her become a lady; he watched the real her emerge and he could not help but to agree that no woman is lesser than the other. As things stand now, he thinks he's going to have a change of mind about announcing his engagement to his current girlfriend after all, all thanks to his mother.

That same night, as Oluchi sat on her bed full of thoughts, she was tempted to call her husband and tell her what she has heard from Martha, but she later lacked the courage. Now she was really confused and doesn't know whether to believe him or Martha. On several occasions, that she had spoken to him he had always pleaded for her patience. According to him, things did not work out the way he had planned; there were certain things he had to put in order before coming home. She had grown to love him and she could not argue with him anytime, they talked. She couldn't wait to set eyes on him, although she was not happy that he had made her wait so long.

Oluchi knew that she cannot have her peace unless she finds out for herself what they have in that room; she remember that before Martha left after their discussion that she has warned her not to leave without finding out for herself, "Don't rely on mere assumptions," she had said.

"Mama pray for your child," she wept, "They won't let me come and see you; pray that I will come home alive."

Love without Flower

She cried herself out and lay quietly thinking of how to go about with her plans. She knew they have two maids, Martha and Fiona, and other male servants. Fiona was the one that she often sees entering the particular room in question, and she doesn't live with the family. She often goes home after each day's work and while Martha stays. She knew quite well that Fiona takes food into the room and that she always wears a particular uniform. She had gone to interrogate her one particular day, but she couldn't get anything from her. Rather, she had told her "she has no clue of what she is talking about." She remembered that she had told her to stop prying into people's affairs, it has sounded like a warning "if I were you, you'd keep to yourself." That night she finally made up her mind to do it, she has to steal Martha's uniform to disguise herself and carry the food to the room by herself; no one would know.

Onyinye Udeh

6

It was a sunny, bright morning, a day that would have been good for a pleasant little walk before having breakfast, except that Oluchi had woken up feeling exhausted, grumpy. She had a rough night and woke at any little noise; so as she dragged herself to the bathroom after her prayers, a thought hit her mind. She smiled to herself and nodded her head in agreement to her thought. She has to do it or she will drive herself insane. She was so much occupied with her plans that for the first time she became a rebel and decided to do things her own way. She agreed it was time she free herself before she would become mad. She wanted to do things the way she liked to do them, so before

Martha could come and call her for breakfast, she was surprised to see that she was not in her room. Oluchi had gone to the kitchen to get her own breakfast, "Let me feel like a human again," she murmured, I cannot enter anywhere, even the kitchen?"

She was there making her tea when she heard a terrible noise; it sounded like the growl of a wounded animal. At that point, Oluchi was scared. *What is it,* she thought, *where is it coming from*? She was so afraid that she quickly dropped her teacup on the floor as she screamed, closing her eyes. She continued screaming, not moving. The mother in-law heard her scream where they were waiting for her to join them at the table and ran to her rescue; on coming there she quickly grabbed her with the help of their maid, and they led her away amidst her questions.

"What was that, did you hear what I've just heard?" Oluchi asked. Nobody had answered her; they only tried to calm her down. The maid had left as soon as she saw that she was calm, while Mrs. Desmond tried to find out what really happened, "You don't have to be afraid," she had said watching her face, "we all heard it."

"You mean you heard it?" Oluchi had asked in surprise.

"Yes dear, but what do you think it was?" Mrs. Desmond asked.

"I don't know but it sounded like a roar, an animal roar?"

"It may be one of these stray dogs" Mrs. Desmond said.

"Maybe," Oluchi said and she seemed to agree, it's nothing. Mrs. Desmond finally concluded as both women laughed at what Oluchi thought was her foolishness. By the time, they finally came for their breakfast, they find out that the men had left, the table was empty; both men had left just as her scream came. They couldn't bear it as they looked at each other. They know where the noise was coming from, and they knew it was junior's voice, trying to communicate. Maybe he was in need. It took the two women by surprise as they looked at each other and as Oluchi was about to blame herself, Mrs. Desmond intervened, "It's okay, let's go on and eat our food, OK. Today, you will accompany me somewhere."

"Me?" Oluchi asked in excitement.

"You mean we are going out; of course, will anyone stop us from going out?" she asked very innocently.

Yes, have you ever seen me step out, even to visit my mother?" She managed to say almost in tears.

"You know things have not worked out the way we planned them. We had this little delay; very soon it's going to be alright."

"I know," Oluchi said, he always tells me so. I can see that you are beginning to be troubled. I understand, and I am willing to help anytime."

"Please don't delay to call on me; you wouldn't want to be sick?" Actually, she felt more relaxed after hearing Mrs. Desmond, but she had suddenly noticed that she too looked sad, and pale, so she was forced to ask, "You are not sick ma, permit me to ask."

"I am okay Oluchi," Mrs. Desmond had hurriedly said; she tried to brighten her face with a smile "hurry up and eat your food."

"What of daddy, won't he object," Oluchi said.

"No, he will not, he will be traveling."

"Oh, I see!" Oluchi said and smiled.

Oluchi had wanted to object when she was told that they will be going just because she has something in her mind. But in a second, she changed her mind; she thought: *Who knows whether I will see someone I know; tomorrow will be the day papa will be away for a whole week, which gives me a lot of time to carry out my plan.* She was happy the way things were working out as she hurried to the bathroom. She could not hide her excitement because she later hurried down the stairs happy that finally she is paying someone a visit. That day eventually became one of the best days she has had since she came to live with the Alex family. Oluchi had so much enjoyed her day that she wished it would always be that way. Mrs. Desmond had taken her to Bar Wilson's house. There she again met Charles after the first time they met at the party. She has forgotten all about him, until now; he was glad to see her again, he could not pretend to have seen how much she has changed as he kept staring at her. Oluchi was happy to meet Mrs. Gloria Oha, Charles' mother as both embraced in greeting; they were glad to see them. When he saw that they have relaxed, he politely took her away, leaving the older women to themselves, "Come and tell me how life has been with you," he said as he led her away.

It was welcomed by the two women. They really needed their own privacy, although on leaving, the mother had told him to treat her with respect; he understood, so he softly smiled. As soon as they were gone, the women poured out their feelings towards the marriage plan. They pitied the poor girl. There Mrs. Desmond openly admits having wronged Oluchi by being part of the plan to marry for a sick man. She should have stood her ground. What if she were my daughter or my niece? She knew she wouldn't have consented to such an arrangement. She made up her mind to keep her busy and happy to save her from being depressed. Meanwhile, Charles had decided to take Oluchi for a little walk in the back yard. She had accepted without any hesitation. She thought within her to enjoy every bit of her stay in the house, the reason was that she doesn't know when such opportunity would come by again.

Later, in the course of their discussion, she learnt from Charles that he would like to see her more often if she was willing. He was afraid to come since the last time they met because he wouldn't know how his father in-law would feel. At first Oluchi had pretended not to hear him, trying to make him drop the subject; but as Charles insisted on getting an answer from her, her countenance began to change as she spoke almost with anger, "Are you making a pass at me, your friend's wife, oh! Stop it, Charles…you all treat me as if I am a widow, why?"

She was beginning to become very angry when Charles intervened; he pleaded for her forgiveness. He never intended to hurt her feelings or disrespect her. "I guess I was carried away, how stupid of me," he lamented, "forget that it happened, I promise it won't repeat itself again."

At that point, they both agreed that it was time they go back. It was already getting dark, so as soon as Oluchi and Charles walked in, Mrs. Desmond announced that they were leaving. They wouldn't want to be late for dinner, so their guest had agreed and was happy to see them off.

On their way home, Oluchi was occupied with thought on whether their outing was a success. Did she have fun as she had expected? *Yes* she said within her, it was one of the most wonderful days she has had, except that Charles nearly messed it up; but come to think of it, *why are they making passes on, when they know that am about to wed? Well,* she thought, *maybe they are carried away nothing serious, beside there is always that temptation whenever a beautiful girl is involved.* She smiled to herself, and then Auntie Margaret, who had pretended not to notice how withdrawn she had looked, decided to ask her how she feels.

"Did you enjoy yourself?" Auntie Margaret asked.

"Oh! I did, auntie; I won't be able to thank you enough. You don't really know what you have done." Oluchi thought it would be nice to share her feelings with Sam, and so as soon as she got home, she went straight to the bar where she expected to find him. Sam could see that she was happy as her face radiated in the light. Oluchi giggled as she told him how happy she felt, and Sam was happy. Sure he likes to see her feeling good and is willing to do anything that will make her happy, he used the opportunity to ask for her forgiveness for acting the way he did and for being angry with her, when he has no right to be. "I wasn't happy with my father when he complained of my being absent from your party."

"Hmm! So why didn't you come, now I remember," Oluchi said.

"Do I have to tell you," Sam asked.

"Of course, I need an explanation," Oluchi replied.

"Okay madam, I didn't come because I am not part of the plan," Sam said.

"You," Oluchi giggled, "you silly boy, you're not part of what? Anyway, where were you that night, out with my friend, your girlfriend?"

"Yes Madam," he said.

"I see," Oluchi said, "I guess I will be meeting her someday."

"I don't think so Oluchi," he answered.

"Why?" she asked looking closely at him.

"Oluchi," Sam called on her, this time holding her hand and looking into her eyes, "a lot has happened since you arrived." He looked somehow worried, good or bad, Oluchi had asked, but then she suddenly changed the topic, she was becoming uncomfortable.

"Sam," she said. "You owe your daddy an apology for not coming to my party."

"I see, okay, if you say so."

Then they both had laughed at their foolish talk. "Sam, I've noticed that you two don't get along very well, why don't you tell about it," Oluchi asked.

"You already have a lot in your mind, I wouldn't want to burden you with my troubles; it's nothing to worry about."

"Okay, if you say so," then she said. "Sam, I miss your brother. I know you do who wouldn't? Do you know that you are strong? Tell me something about him."

She looked straight into his eyes, and then Sam paused; he seemed to gather himself before speaking, "He is kind. He would never hurt you. Are you happy now?" he asked looking at her smiling, at her innocence.

"Yes, Sam, I am," she said smiling, too. Actually, Sam was beginning to get nervous not knowing the direction their discussion would go, but Oluchi was so happy to have noticed, so on seeing that, he decided to play along with her; he would hate to be the one to spoil her fun. That night, after their long talk, Oluchi was still giggling as Sam led her towards her room. She wished that it would never end as Sam later wished her good night. Oluchi entered her room and then realized how late it was, 9 p.m. on the dot. She was so happy and full and didn't notice that they had missed their dinner. She was beginning to feel tired when she decided just to lie down and rest a little before taking off her clothes, but she had quickly slept off as soon as her head touched the pillow.

She was suddenly awakened by banging and whispering and some sort of noise. At first she had thought that it was a nightmare only to realize that it was a storm, a strong wind, blowing and banging against her window. She realized that in the course of her excitement, she forgot to lock her windows and change herself. She hurried to shut the window against the flapping of the curtain. Then she hurriedly changed her clothes and went back to sleep, but she hardly slept when she realized that it was morning already. Then the thought rushed back to her mind. She has a very important assignment to carry out. The storm was stronger now as she looked through her window. It was beginning to get dark, and the clouds had already gathered, a sign that it's going to rain. *It's going to be a stormy one* she thought, the clashing of the thunder indicates that; it made her shiver a little, "I wouldn't want the thunder to disturb my peace," she said to herself. So before coming down to have her breakfast, she ran around to make sure that all doors and windows were properly shut. *She needed her peace to perfect what she wants to do* she thought

7

So after the breakfast, she saw that all had left except for the maids and Mrs. Desmond, she quickly ran into her room as she noticed that the time was approaching for the maid to carry in the food. She changed her clothes, to look exactly like one of the maids. Instead of waiting for the exact time, she went one hour ahead of the exact time so that before the maid would have come by, she would be through with her plans; she wouldn't want anything to spoil it. She hardly slept last night because she was very anxious. Oluchi hurried down the stairs quietly, and every little noise seemed to startle her, but she managed to keep her calm. Seeing that no one was around, she grabbed the key from where it was kept, and carried the already prepared food on the tray and headed towards the room.

Her heartbeat was so fast that she was at the edge of collapsing; she felt like going back, *but she have to do it* she thought, *if not I won't be able to have my peace.* When she walked away from the corridor and from everyone's possible prying eyes, she hurried towards the door and gently placed the tray on the floor. She hurriedly took out the key, opened the door and was about to slip in when she suddenly changed her mind, *there is no use for all this* she thought It's not worth it, *suppose there is someone's corpse, what am I going to do when I find out, this is all wrong, after all my life has been at their mercy since I came and nothing has happened. I might as well stay and see the end of it.*

Having decided against carrying out her plans, she hurried back to keep all that she had taken before someone finds out, and she prayed for her silly self. As soon as she saw that she was in her room and no one had suspected or seen anything, Oluchi heaved a sigh of relief as she sat on her bed; she waited to recover her breath and seeing that all the nervousness had stopped, she decided it was time to take a hot bath. The thought had kept coming, but Oluchi had determined to suppress it. She had to hold herself together and let things unfold by themselves, but she never waited long, not long after that incident all her questions were answered.

Onyinye Udeh

8

It was on one particular evening, a day that had seemed like every other day she had spent since she arrived. That day she had gone riding with her mother-in-law on their property. It was such a huge property that it stretched so far you could only see the one at the other end with a help of binoculars. And so by the time they were through and riding back home, she was happy and feeling relaxed. She was so happy that as they entered the house, she hardly noticed the presence of her father-in-law. He was standing at the entrance, with a half-smile on his face; it was his voice that startled Oluchi, "I can see that you've enjoyed your riding, my dear?"

"Oh! Yes, papa," Oluchi said. She looked so excited you could easily see it on her face.

"I am sorry I didn't see you," she apologized.

"It's okay, dear, come along with me," he continued as he gently took her hand, trying to lead her away. "I have an important issue to discuss with you, your auntie may leave us now," he said while coming closer to where his wife was standing. He kissed her on the cheek.

Oluchi didn't expect meeting him there, it looked like he was purposely waiting for her, and so as Mrs. Desmond excused herself; he led her inside the house, leading her to the same path she has passed through few days ago. Her heartbeat suddenly increased, just few days ago, when she had gone through that path, she had wanted to take the law into her own hands. *Now here it is* she thought, *but what is it that he wants to show me there, is there something there really, what did he wants to do with me in the room, so the rumor is true, is he going to sacrifice me oh!* She was beginning to tremble when she decided to calm herself; she would'nt want him to find out, what reason would she give?

She was still battling with that thought when she heard him call, "Oluchi, I know you would be wondering what it might be that I want to discuss with you," he softly said, looking closely at her. "I guess it is time to get it over with. My dear, I am about to take you on a journey that you will never forget as long as you live."

Oluchi never said a word, the way things look, it's like her contribution was not needed, so she quietly listened as her heart pounded away.

"It is a short journey," he continued, "what I may call the journey of your life; it may sound strange, but it's true. I only wish that one day in your life, you will find a place in your heart to forgive me."

Now he looked troubled, his countenance had changed to that of a man in sorrow.

"Oluchi, do you remember the day I told you not to enter a particular room in this house?"

She nodded, she couldn't speak. She was fighting to steady herself. She was dying of curiosity, almost out of her mind.

"I think it's time I tell you why I told you not to go in there; suppose I tell you that my son is not abroad. Suppose I tell you that since he was 8 years old, he has not walked out from his room by himself. Suppose I tell you that he is a sick man, and that he had been in this house since you came, that he is the one lying helpless in that same room that I told you not to enter."

Oluchi had heard enough; she couldn't get hold of herself, she slumped as he introduced her to his son. It didn't come as a surprise to him. He had expected it and therefore had prepared for it. Their family doctor was there in the room together with Mrs. Desmond; they had all waited for the worst. She had known what her husband's plan was, so she had to be there to lend a hand. Sir Alex was heartbroken when he saw Oluchi faint; the wife had quickly come to his rescue and took him away as the doctor attended to her. *It was all over* he thought as he lay quietly on his bed trying to gather himself. He felt more relieved now; he had never felt what he feels now since Oluchi came, *and whatever happens now is the least that can happen* he thought.

The very day Oluchi reported that Sam had made advances on her to Mrs. Desmond, she was troubled. She knew that it was time they tell her the truth. She had never had her peace since Oluchi came, knowing what lay ahead. What if she decided to make trouble? What if she fall sick? While waiting endlessly, things had gotten out of hand since her husband refused to disclose their secret earlier. He thought it will be better to tell her when she had grown to love the family, but it didn't work out. Instead, it had made her more curious and anxious. She was becoming hysterical each day that passed. Mrs. Desmond knew that something had to be done before things got out of hand. *An elder doesn't stay in the house while the she goat delivers in its tethered* she thought, *that's the words of our elders.* The possibility of sexual temptations cannot be avoided, knowing that her husband was sick, she had no one to protect her. So she had gone along to make her husband listen to her, "You've not considered how much your reputation is at stake if these should be known, it's going to bring you down, can you survive it. After these long years of hard work, seeing your name in every leading newspaper, making headlines of kidnapping, that's what it is, again don't forget that she is someone's child, you can imagine the plight of her mother…" She was about breaking down when her husband drew her to himself.

"It's okay now," he said. "I've never seen you cry, I will do as you say."

Oluchi was quickly revived but was still in shock; they feared the worse for her as days passed and she was still delirious, calling her mother once in a while as tears streamed down her eyes. At first they thought of going to their home for her mom, then on a second thought, it was canceled. What if she comes and dies herself? Those few weeks were such tough ones that they also feared for Sir Alex's life; he has refused to come and see her because he couldn't stand it. Auntie Margaret had never taken a sleeping pill, but she had pleaded with their doctor to prescribe one for her, so everything had suddenly come to a halt. They waited helplessly, fearing the worst as they watched the doctor do his best, but eventually she pulled through.

Oluchi recovered and all were happy, happy that no life was lost. She barely eats, cried most of the time, and refused to say a word. They could see that she was sad. The very day Sir Alex went to see her, in her recovery room, he told her the pathetic story of his life.

"I married your auntie, when my first wife died, leaving me and my son. Then it was difficult for me to accept it because I thought I couldn't live without her; but after the days of mourning was over and life had returned to normal, I devoted my life to my work and my little boy. I believed that one day we would all be happy, but such a day never came. Then I enrolled my son in the best, most costly, school in the country. I wanted to do all that is within my power to see him succeed, but I guess fate has another plan for him.

Onyinye Udeh

As little as he was then, 8 years old at that time, he was already rooted in the music. I will not forget the day they had their music concert at his school. I could remember proudly pointing at him as my son. I couldn't hold my excitement as I watched him perform, but after that day, he never stepped out from his room on his feet again. I would like to say that as soon as my wife died, the enemy entered my family. It all started after his mother's death. I had cried and refused to be comforted, and, as a result, have a nervous breakdown that took me months to get back on my feet again. During this period my son, unnoticed by me, was pining away in fear anytime he saw me collapse. Suddenly, he will leave whatever he was doing and scream for help; so even when I was recovering he was would be terrified to be with me. He lost confidence that I would ever be normal again.

Eventually, when I was fully recovered, happy that am up again, I noticed that my son was beginning to be scared, at times shivering with fear. So I did not waste time in consulting a doctor. I remember he came to my house for a thorough examination. According to the doctor, my son had been traumatized by my illness, and he provided a prescription for him and told me that he needed some rest; but as I was seeing him off, he added that he needed someone who would be very close to him all the time, a mother he had bluntly said. When I realized that it had come to a matter of life and death, I decided it was time I get married. I can do everything to save my son's life, but life would never be the same again.

One morning, as I sat on the couch reading my paper, I felt someone's presence; and, on looking up, I saw Alex in his pajamas clutching on the curtain. Looking closely at him, I could see that he was shaking. He was standing in front of his bedroom, unable to move; he was trying to call me, but he could not. Seeing him in that condition, I was terrified as I ran to help him. I quickly carried him while calling for help, and then my wife and other members of the family came to my rescue. We took him to the hospital, and at first the doctors thought it was post-encephalitic, an acute inflammation of the brain based on the symptoms he was having: fever, drowsiness, fatigue. But after running several tests without positive results, it was ruled out.

It was found out that my son has developed a rare illness that has no diagnosis or cure; his health had kept deteriorating. I did all I could to bring him to normal again, but all failed. When I saw that the doctors in our country could no longer do it, I decided to take him overseas for more proper treatment, but still his condition had continued to get worse. He lost his sense of hearing, talking, seeing, utterly incompetent. Then the tears have started flowing down his cheeks. You can imagine the plight of a father as I helplessly watch my son vanish.

He groaned, turning his face away from her….neither my wife nor has my son tasted my wealth. I called for help and found known, I watch my son in pity as he withdraw to an unknown world. That was when I hated life. My money could not give me happiness. My hope in my son was shattered in my presence. I had thought that one day, he would grow to control my empire, but I was left with nothing. That was when I vowed that no one will take his place in my heart. I vowed that whatever I will do for my normal child, I will do even more for him; he paused as Oluchi tried to wipe away his tears. He had always played tough, but this time around he couldn't fight it.

Oluchi, too, could not control her feelings. She let the tears flow, she could now see why he never laughed; she was totally broken as she watched the elderly man try to control his tears. She could easily despair.

"Now that you have known his voice had startled her, I don't know your plans, but you are not leaving," he snarled.

"Why," Oluchi cried, "Why? Don't you see that there is nothing to be done?" She muttered amidst tears.

"There is. The doctor said he needed love. That is the only medicine; he may not be himself, but I know that wherever his mind is he can understand the strong power of love. He needs someone to call his own that's the way I see it."

Oluchi had sobbed and could not control her emotions when Sir Alex left. Right now she was too tired to act, but her mind was filled with thought. "I see," she muttered, "now I know the reason for all the bitterness in him. Oh God, help us!" she cried as she sobbed; the woman of the house was beside her, trying to calm her down.

"I hope you don't mind all that he had said," she gently asked her. "He never meant it; he loves you, not only because of his son, he may not be willing to show it, but I know he does."

"But all hope is not lost," Oluchi said watching her carefully. "He has another son."

"You mean my son?" Auntie Margaret asked.

"His son," Oluchi corrected, "his stepson. Oh! I see. I see why they don't get along; most men are like that anyway."

"Yes, he sees Sam as a threat to Alex," Auntie Margaret replied. ;

"It's OK, he is a sick man," Oluchi finally said.

"I had my son as a single mother and then I was his legal adviser. My son was only a child when we became part of his life, but up till now they see each other as strangers. I am so sorry we have to cause you this trouble," she pleaded. "We were not a part of the plan to marry for Alex, but what can we do?" She paused, looking for her reaction. "That had been his quarrel with Samuel recently; please forgive us, I promise you from now on you are free to do as you wish."

It had all been a devastating discovery for Oluchi. Anytime she was alone in her room, her mind would go back to that very day when she actually met her husband to be. "Is that what she had gotten herself into?" She will ask herself. What she thought was her dawn had become her sorrow. For the first time in her life, she remembered her father, how she wished he were alive. What would people say if they heard that her so-called overseas husband is a sick man? Why did God allow it, is there a reason for that? She didn't imagine it; there is no way she could have imagined in a million years that her husband, was actually in the same house with her. She had thought just like everyone else that Sir Alex is an occultist. In this present world, it is not difficult to say that he has used his son for occult purpose that had been the belief of the people. The gossip had been such since she had arrived, but now she knows better.

That day she can remember seeing him struggle with death, uncontrollable body movements; she couldn't see more for she had passed out. She was already gone even before she came face to face with him. She learnt later that what she had thought was an animal growl, the day she threw her cup of tea on the floor, was the voice of her hus…she could not bring herself to say the word that had been his only speech. It was all arranged, the man who she had spoken with on phone, the constant postponing of her husband's homecoming; *that is why Sam was tempted to make passes on her,* she thought; *he sees her as not having any man.* She also found out that Fiona is a nurse and not a maid, and then there were the dreams. Yes, she remembers they were two, but one had kept repeating itself, and nearly turned into a nightmare.

She will not forget the dream she had the very day she first slept in that house. That very night the party was over and she was glad that finally she could now go to her room, have her bath and enjoy a good night's sleep. She had been so exhausted from the long trip that she could drop dead if care were not taken. She has done exactly as she had thought and with the help of her maid, everything went fast. She lay down to sleep after saying her prayers and quickly drifted away, and then she had a dream, in that dream she saw herself ready for her wedding. She was looking gorgeous in her wedding gown, standing closer to the entrance of the church, and waiting for her bridal train, beaming all over with smiles.

Her husband, was already in the church, waiting. They finally arrived and marched closer to where she was standing. In that dream it was a little boy who had her bouquet, and then the little boy, on reaching where she was standing, lifted his hand, to hand over the flowers, but the bouquet fell from his hand to the floor. He stood there looking confused, but not making any effort to pick it up. Upon seeing what had happened, she had quickly bent over to pick it up, but on touching it, the petals kept falling off, breaking apart. It felt as if she were touching ashes. In any case, she tried to manage and gather it, but it dissolved in her hand; her hand was a mess, but she kept trying to pick it until finally she awakened.

She had several times wondered what the dream might mean, but she couldn't come up with anything. Now she understands, the little-confused boy was Alex, the same age he was when his sickness started. It was that innocent stage, his spirit was still very young, although he had grown to be a man. He was the petal that had kept falling apart, messing up her hand; now that she had seen her husband and see how bad his condition looked, she is left with nothing.

And then there was this other dream. In this particular dream, she saw herself wearing a man's shirt; it was a little bigger than her, an oversize shirt. Later, when she took off the shirt, she was horrified to see that she had sustained a very big deep wound. One side of her chest down to her lungs had been eaten. It looked like a wound sustained from a carnivorous animal. Her flesh was torn in pieces, damaged and dangling from her body, in shreds. It was a startling discovery to her because she didn't know she had a wild animal hidden in the shirt; she never saw one, she didn't feel any pain when it was eating her. She only realized what had happened when she took off the shirt. It had made her fearful, fearful of the unknown. What does it mean for her flesh to be torn in shreds, the wound in her heart? Actually, that was the reason for her crying the day the Alex family came to take her with them, although she decided to tell her people that it was because they were strangers. She never wanted to upset anyone. Now everything is clear, her marriage had caused her sorrow, and her heart was torn in pieces. The wound would always be there, yes, Sir Alex was right; it is the journey of her life, the journey she would never forget as long as she lives. Actually, God was trying to communicate with her, but she was not sensitive. *If only we could focus more on the things of the spirit,* she thought, *where everything is bare and nothing is a secret.*

9

As Oluchi slowly recovered, she knew that she couldn't stay; she could now understand why Sam had told her to leave. This is something she had not prepared for, not that she cannot cope with the condition of the young man. After all, he had been taken care of by someone; his condition is such that no one would like to turn their back against him without helping. But she would not stay because his father was not truthful to her, and to her people; he deceived her, she had to leave. She did not hesitate to tell her father-in-law her plans, but on hearing them, he became angry. "You are not leaving," he snarled, groaning at the same time.

"Oh, I did everything for you! What is it that you want? How could I be happy?" Oluchi answered back. "How could I be thankful for the flashy gifts you showered on me, when… when it was all lies?" she sobs. "You deceived me; you took advantage of my condition. You couldn't have come to me, if not that your son is sick," she screamed. "I came to marry and not to be given gifts. I've already built a strong love for your son, believing that one day he would come to me, but now I see that am left with nothing, my love is without flower!. If only he could hear me." She then cried.

All the time that Oluchi was talking, Sir Alex had listened patiently without any interruption, but when she was through, he softly replied to her, "I have no excuse for what I have done; I guess I overstepped my boundary. You may be right to say that I took advantage of your background, but let me remind you that I've not been going around begging for any girl I see, to marry my son. I couldn't have come to you if I have not seen you and loved you."

When he said that Oluchi's eyes sparkled with surprise. "Yes," he responded to her stare, "I wanted the best for my son; so when Theophilus told me he has someone for my son, I insisted on seeing the person in question. I refused to accept pictures because they could be deceitful, but then he suddenly came up with the idea of taking your video, the day your local government chairman did a rally in your village. You were there with your mother that was the day.

"Again, I was once poor like you. I didn't acquire my wealth overnight. I have struggled with my wife for several years before we were able to have our breakthrough. But then what happened, she died without tasting it. On that day I had hurried home to tell my wife that I've just been paid for my first contract job, I couldn't wait to see her reaction when she set eyes on the money in the briefcase I carried; but instead, on arriving home, I met her lying on the bed. I had thought I would meet her with our boy, or in the kitchen, but still I never suspected anything as I gently placed the briefcase on the bed and opened it for her to see. 'Touch it honey' I said laughing, 'touch it, this is money.' In the course of my excitement, I couldn't notice that she was sick, I noticed when I wanted to lift her hand to place it on the money, and her temperature was above normal, very hot. I couldn't understand as I cried, why now, why now! She was taken to the hospital and they said she has a weak heart, she never recovered, one year after my breakthrough she died, we all have our trouble my dear, I hate to make it seem that I want to be pitied but that is how it is, kindly bear with me."

On hearing that, Oluchi felt for him, she agreed that actually "life is not complete for anyone."

10

Before the day Oluchi announced her departure, Sam had come home and heard that she had found out the truth. He had traveled on a business trip and was not around when the whole thing was happening. While he was away, he had tried several times to reach Oluchi to find how she was doing, but she didn't answer. Then he had decided to call his mother, as maybe she would be able to tell him why Oluchi wouldn't pick, but it scared him when his mother didn't answer her phone, too. He was tempted to call his father, but he canceled the idea. He wouldn't want anything that would put him in a state of panic. He knew that all was not well and decided to hurry with the remaining things he had to do before boarding an available flight home.

While he was seated in the plane, he tried to imagine why they had ignored his calls. He couldn't come up with anything, so he decided to flip through the magazines to distract his mind as he traveled. So as soon as their plane landed, he boarded an airport taxi and headed home. On reaching home he hurried inside the house in anticipation of meeting his family, but no one was there; the parlor was empty and quiet, so as his tension mounted, and he was about to call out for someone's attention, he met their family doctor. The doctor was coming down the stairs. Upon seeing him, Sam had stopped and was staring at his face searching for a clue. Then the doctor spoke, when he saw how worried Sam had looked.

"It's okay Sam. I can see you're just coming back. I came to see your mother; she has had a rough week. It's nothing Sam. She is in her room resting. She will tell you everything you want to know."

Sam had hurried up the stairs to her mum's room and met her lying on her bed; she looked terrible. As soon as her mother saw the look on Sam's face, she tried to brighten her face, telling him that all is well, and that was how he learnt about it. Sam, on hearing how it all happened, loved that she had known the truth but still feared the worst. He knows that his father can be stubborn, and he may not allow her to leave if she wants to. He had thought, so even before going to see Oluchi, he had gone to talk things over with his father. On meeting him, he gently told him what he thought would be the best decision to make. If she wants to go wish her well, let her decide for herself; he thought his father would like to think it over, but instead he was offended. Sam was not surprised, he had expected it; he wants to know whose order it was, and Sam had lovingly told him that it was not an order. He had only come to help, but when he saw that his effort to make him reason had failed, and then it was his turn to be angry.

"I wanted to make things easy for all of us, but you always see me as nothing; you have forced us before but not again…Can't you reason that this is kidnapping, keeping someone's child against her will."

"Against whose will?" Sir Alex demanded. "Did she tell you that she wants to leave? You talk as if you are sure, let me correct you young man, I did not kidnap her; the day I went to her family and completed every marriage rite, paid the bride price that day she became part of this family, Mrs.

Oluchi Alex Desmond that's who she is! She's my son's wife, understand!"

"You're right dad. I am only saying that she has to make that decision herself," Sam said.

Sam then stormed out of his father's room; he was so angry that it clearly showed on his face. The house was so hot for everyone, and things seemed to have stopped moving from that day of confrontation onwards. There were so much disagreement and raising of voices. So when Sam and his mother heard Oluchi scream, they thought that she had screamed on the account of her experience; so they went to see what it was and met her with their father. They knew what it was although they were not there when it started. Then Mrs. Desmond had gently led Oluchi away to her own room as Sam tried to talk to his daddy, but both men fell apart, they couldn't stand each other's attitude anymore. There was nothing they withheld from each other, and it became so hot that Mrs. Desmond was tempted to call a friend for help. But out of rage on seeing her, Sir Alex hurried to where she was and tried to snatch the phone. Their son, seeing how angry he looked, thought that he was about to hit her and hurried to stop him, grabbing him from behind. That's when he collapsed in his arms.

It was heartbreaking as Sam looked closely at him and saw how tired and worn-out, he looked; *the situation has wearied him* he thought, *how I wish he will take me as his son.* He sobbed. Mrs. Desmond has already attracted the attention of the household, Oluchi, too, on hearing voices and cries, had come running down the stairs. She saw as they carried him away and broke into tears, walking back to her room. She could not bear to see father and son in tears, "When is she leaving?" he kept mumbling as he lay on his bed. "I have…come to love her as a daughter I never had. Please help me."

They called the doctor as soon he was on the bed, and all prayed that he would come through. It was like a gloomy shadow was hanging on their family. They had thought that all was well when Oluchi recovered, but now, it's their father. It's like someone must pay with his or her life before they would finally have their peace.

As they waited restlessly for the day Oluchi would announce her departure, mother and son had secretly agreed that they would see that Oluchi stays for some time until Sir Alex was on his feet again; they didn't want to lose him. It was time they straightened out everything and made him enjoy his remaining days on earth.

But she did not leave, after seeing what happened, she felt for the family, for her father- in-law and mostly for Alex. She made up her mind to stay. She wanted to share their grief with them. She wanted to put a smile on their faces, reconciling father and son before she leaves. Lastly, she wanted to show love to her husband, who she came to marry and she would do it. Nothing mattered to her anymore, what people would say; it was her life and no one would define it for her. They didn't expect it when she finally told them. Sam had thought she was out of her mind; he had paused on hearing her decision, staring at her closely before saying a word, "You amaze me all the time," he softly said. "Are you sure this is what you want? You really amaze me, if that is what you want then I give you my support."

The father-in-law had expected her to be leaving, but he was overwhelmed with joy when he learnt her change of mind. "When are you leaving?" he had asked the day Oluchi came to see how he was doing. She had slowly waved her head, "I am not leaving," she said smiling. "I am staying with my husband." It was all joy, but Oluchi's joy was not complete.

As things returned to normal, Oluchi was no more in haste; she had decided to stay and that was final. She thought on how her mother would react to the news when she finds out everything that had happened. How would life be for her? She was planning on taking a trip to her hometown, when one afternoon, Sir Alex called her into his study and told her to prepare for home.

"You have to go and see your mother, I've wronged her, too," he softly said. She slowly looked at him, as she was not excited anymore about going home. She would have loved to call her first to at least hear her voice, but there was no way of communicating with her by phone. She had to make haste and pay her a visit, but as she was about to leave the room, her father-in-law held her hand as her tears dropped; he pulled her closer and held her in a warm embrace. "Forgive me," he looked very ashamed as he spoke softly to her, "I know I have wronged you. I have had enough trouble in this life that I think I needed help." He sorrowfully told her that he did not mean to cause her any sorrow.

11

Oluchi did not stay another night in their house. She had done as their father said, to go and see her mother. But then, Sam had paid her a visit in her room. She was lying quietly on her bed trying to gather herself together after talking with her father-in-law. That's when she heard a knock at her door, and before she was able to rise from her bed and drag herself to the door, Sam opened it and stepped in.

This was the first time that both were seeing since Sam returned; she didn't say anything but stared closely at him. She looked straight to Sam and seemed to ask, *why, even you*? But then she let it pour out as Sam closed his arm around her. "Yes, you can beat me if you want to; we all dragged you into the mess, but I am sorry that we have caused you such pain. Its better you let it out. It's going to be all right."

She nodded at every word until she was quiet again. Both had stayed and talked more before Sam finally left, but then she was relieved because he had promised to help her on her journey. The next day as she traveled, she felt alive again; the father-in-law had strongly supported her, and she had everything that she wanted. Sam took her to the airport himself and saw that she boarded the plane before he finally came back

She was thinking of staying for only a few days, but on reaching home and seeing how bad her mother's condition had become, she had a change of mind. So they had hastily left the following day. Oluchi's mother was almost out of her mind when she returned. Though she had recognized her daughter when she saw her, but there were no feelings as if she was no more the one she had cried and waited for, and then Oluchi could not take it. She cried and refused to be comforted. What she thought would be a moment of joy had turned to that of mourning.

The family members had thought that her cry was as a result of her mother's illness, but that was not it at all; her journey of life had made her bitter. Oluchi was happy to see her people again, and they were glad to see that she was alive and had not forgotten them. She learnt that after she had failed to communicate with them, they had made every effort to contact her; her mother and her uncle had on their own gone to the city to look for her. It was when they failed to make any contact that they alerted the villagers. A search party was sent again to the city and again they failed to bring any positive report back. The villagers excommunicated Theo's father when he failed to produce his son's phone number. It was then that her mother became ill. She kept to herself and refused to eat. They took her to the local hospital, but she kept going down, and she slowly became more depressed.

Oluchi's mother later recovered, but it was in the city. Uncle Julius had supported her decision to take her to the city for proper treatment. He was glad to see that she was not lost as they had feared. She was tempted to break the news of her marriage to her at the village, but after narrating her ordeal to her uncle, who she had met in the name of marriage, it really touched him; he wanted to involve his kinsmen on how to tackle the issue, but Oluchi had refused the idea.

"I wanted to tell you so you know why I didn't come back as planned, but I have made up my mind to stay," Oluchi said.

The elderly man looked closely at her and smiled. "You have grown my daughter. I am going to support you. We are brave people and we don't quit when the going gets tough. So, if this is what you want, then I give you my blessing, but for now we don't have to tell mama. You will tell her when she is recovered in the city. That was how they kept it from her until she was fully recovered. She had cried and cursed Sir Alex and his family; they didn't take any offense. They deserved more than a curse. Sir Alex had pleaded that he would make it up with her, and they finally managed to calm her down. She was eager to see the sick young man, but her daughter would not let her. Finally, when she later did, all hell broke loose again; she vowed that her daughter was leaving with her, but before she leaves she had to go and tell his people because she will not let Sir Alex go unpunished.

But then she was shocked when Oluchi told her that she was staying. "What!?" She had screamed. Oluchi told her mother that Alex junior is her husband and…She didn't let her finished as she snapped at her, "Which Alex," she shouted, "the dead one or the living one?"

"Mama, I know you are angry and I understand whether he's dead or alive, he is still my husband. Don't forget, you all married me to him. Remember what our people say she playfully said to her mother, "Marriage is like a parcel, you take whatever you find in it." "I hope you've not allowed him to touch you? " How I wish he can, Oluchi responded." "You silly child, come to your mother." And that is how the issue of leaving or not leaving ended.

In the course of Amoge's stay, she saw how close Sam had been to her daughter and it pleased her. So one evening, as they were about to retire, she told her what she has observed. Oluchi pretended that she didn't know what she was saying, but she failed to give up.   "Listen to me. You don't have to go unrewarded, you have to be smart; if he wants you, accept him. You can even elope with him if he is willing. I already give you my blessing," Amoge said.

"It's okay, mama, you are sick. Don't forget that I am not a widow yet," Oluchi said.

She finally accepted things as they were when she saw that her daughter had made up her mind.

Onyinye Udeh

12

Oluchi said she would stay and she did. They saw it in her deeds. From the moment, it came out from her mouth, she took major responsibility of taking care of her husband. Although the nurse was always there to help, Oluchi was always there feeding him, talking to him, and making sure that he was very comfortable. However, prior to that time, she had gone to see him, and took a proper look on how he actually looked. That was the day she saw clearly how bad his condition really was. That day she had gone in company of her father-in-law, she felt she would be better off with him alone, because she wanted her privacy. After all, it was her life and it was high time she took charge of it. Although she was anxious on whether she would be able to get hold of herself, the thought of going into that room again kept reminding her of the ordeal she passed through a few weeks ago. Yet, she was determined to go, it had come to her and she was not going to run away.

It was on a Sunday morning that they went. They walked down the corridor as she had feared, but her father-in-law kept encouraging her when he noticed that she was a little nervous. They made it to the door and Sir Alex led her in, towards where his son was. At first Oluchi was speechless as she watched him fight for his life; his eyes were open, but there was no sign of life in them. Oluchi spotted a little movement once in a while, and heard what sounded like groaning. Oluchi went closer to him and kissed him on the forehead, and then sat on the chair closer to him. She called to him as she held his hand in hers, "Alex, my Alex, what happened to you? What would you tell mama when you will finally meet her? Will you say that as soon as she turned her back, you followed because you were afraid…because you couldn't fight? Don't you know that the world is a battleground? Why did you quit, why!?"

Now she was sobbing, with tears running down her cheeks. Sir Alex stood up from where he was sitting and went towards the window; he didn't want her see his tears. Her words had seemed to bring back all the bitter memories he had.

"Why didn't you fight, Alex," she called out as if he were hearing her. "Do you know that I once fought for my life? I guess my life is made up of stories, as long as I can remember, I've been fighting for my life. Once I was dying of food poisoning. I had eaten a poisonous mushroom while I was trying to survive; but I fought, even when I saw that I was dying, my hands were twisting but I held on; why didn't you fight? Alex, can you hear me? Why did you bring me here to break my heart, is that a no! No, big boys don't break their loved one's heart."

So she cried and wept, and Sir Alex was forced to take her away from the room. Oluchi touched the very heart of Sir Alex, and so from time to time he laughs, although he still doesn't get along with his stepson. He has seen that he has an interest in Oluchi and it made him sad. He had called him privately and told him to keep away from her. Sam did not argue. He knows that what he was saying was true; he had fallen in love with her. He had a girlfriend before, but since he started having feelings toward Oluchi, things didn't seem to work out. Again, he had tried to force himself several times, but was not working. He hadn't planned it, but it had happened. He had to find a solution soon. He needed someone to talk to, someone who could advise him; so he went to his friend Charles, but he soon realized that Charles

Love without Flower

was beginning to like Oluchi, too. Sam was angry and decided to leave quickly. *Now I know why he always call to know how she was faring*, he thought; he warned Charles before leaving never to speak it out.

13

When Sam saw that Oluchi has decided to stay even though her joy was limited, he felt for her. *How could she be happy when her husband is ill?* He thought; it was a tough decision that she had made, but as he promised, he would support her. So one afternoon, he forced her out from the house and took her to the beach; there he opened his heart to her, told him everything about himself and the problem he had been having with his girlfriend all because of her. Oluchi had laughed, and told him to be careful lest she gives him a hot water bath; both had laughed at the joke. They were all alone for the first time and they loved it. Oluchi was not angry anymore with Sam for openly expressing how he felt towards her. She didn't want him to feel guilty. She still had a man in her life and she would always love him. She then pleaded with Sam to try and make peace with his father and he agreed; they were happy riding home after their picnic, but it was all shattered when they reached home and met their father. He had come back and could not find Oluchi.

All hell broke loose when he learnt that Sam had taken her to the beach, he shouted at his wife and angrily waited for their return. It was sad when they later came back because he slapped him so hard and warned him not to repeat it. Sam was sad; he couldn't control his anger; things were getting out of hand he thought. His plan was to leave the house, but Oluchi and her mother had pleaded with him. Oluchi was not happy, either. He didn't deserve it she thought; she tried to bring peace between the two, but she had failed.

14

Today was a very special day in the family of Sir Alex Desmond. It is always his tradition to celebrate his son's birthday. Oluchi had not been part of it until it came around again. Sir Alex had prepared to make it more special since all was working well as he had planned. As he thought, Alex had not been able to be present at his birthday, now he had someone to represent him. He would be proud to show off his son's beautiful wife. But on that very day as the celebration was going on, Oluchi suddenly went upstairs when she felt that the party was in full swing. She, too, had her own special plan. They had suddenly felt her absence and thought maybe she had gone to refresh herself, but just as they were laughing and chatting, they suddenly felt a hush. Soon all stood still, looking in one particular direction. At first Sir Alex hadn't noticed anything as he laughed, but when he saw his friends' attention directed to a place he was forced to look. He looked and he quickly dropped his glass of wine. Sam, on seeing her, had gone to help; he, too, was taken aback, as he saw her wheel his brother towards the parlor. Their father was in rage, "You fool! Who told you to bring him here?"

"Nobody told me," Oluchi said, gently leaving the wheelchair and facing him. "For years you've kept him bound in one place like an animal," she too snarled, "you never wanted anyone to see him…you are ashamed to show off your son just because he is sick!"

He couldn't stand it anymore; he could not bear it as he screamed, Stop! Stop it!"

His face turned away from her, he told her that she was hurting him. She told him that now he had no control over his sick son.

"But he is my son," he shouted.

"And he is my husband," she replied. "Or have you forgotten? Now I make decisions for him. I know that if he were in his right sense, he would not be in his room while they celebrate his birthday!"

"But I love my son," he groaned.

"I love him, too, papa; and I love you," she said. She then warmly embraced her father-in-law. "Forgive me, I didn't mean to hurt anyone. I felt for once let him have a breath of fresh air."

The crowd stood still and watched; that day they saw a different side of Sir Alex as he wept

15

It was not long after his birthday that young Alex quietly died in his room. That very day the wife had gone as usual to attend to his needs and found him dead. She had screamed and they all came running to his room. On seeing what had happened, the mother-in-law had led her away from the room as Sam and his father cried over the deceased, "I know it, Sir Alex cried; he had waited for someone who would love him, someone who would mourn him when he was gone. She did it," he laughed and cried at the same time.

At the burial Oluchi confessed that he had won as she read the funeral oration, "As his father had wished, it had happened to him, he had love; he came and said goodbye to all his friends the day I took him out of his room. Nothing shall trouble him anymore, goodnight my sweetheart. It was touching, and people were unable to hold their tears. Oluchi's mother was there, the father-in-law groaned within him, but he was satisfied on how it all ended. Although he still feared that Oluchi might decide to leave, and he had grown to love her as his own daughter. He was ready to adopt her. Sam had wasted no time in telling her his plans, how he feels towards her, and her mother was pestering her, either Sam or Charles, but she was not leaving here empty-handed.

16

When the burial and mourning were over, Oluchi, too was happy the way it ended. She was happy to have stayed. She was happy that she didn't quit as she wouldn't have forgiven herself if she had left. She was proud of herself. She heard all that everybody had to say; she loved Sam, he had been the Alex she knew since she first arrived. Charles, too, was not bad, but she was not in a hurry to get married right away.

"I will go and come back. Anyone that has waited for me I will marry," Oluchi said.

When Sam heard her decision, he knew she was right again; she needed a rest and also time to think. He, too, decided it was time he left his mother, so that she could enjoy her marriage.

As Oluchi prepared to leave, Sam was preparing as well. He couldn't stay in that house without Oluchi. Sir Alex had known she will leave, she has done her work. *Nothing is holding her anymore,* he thought, but he still believed that he could make her stay. She had tasted another side of life and wasn't worth going back. He also wanted to stop Sam, but could he? When his son died, he realized that he needed another son. *I am getting old now, who would take care of my life when I am old, or who would continue where I stopped when I am gone?* He thought. Now he knew it, he needs Sam.

Again, he realized that he had wronged him so much, and he wouldn't like him to leave feeling hurt, but his pride would not let him give in. He wanted to go and plead with him when his wife informed him that he was leaving. But on that particular day, he couldn't stand to see him leave. Oluchi had despite his plea although she promised she would always be a part of his family. *The house was becoming empty* he thought. "My son," he cried, as Sam was about to leave, "you will not leave me!" Sam didn't need him to say anymore. Sir Alex had never called him his son. It all settled

Love without Flower

the longtime disagreement between them, as father and son grabbed each other in a warm embrace.

The end.

Onyinye Udeh

About The Author

Mrs. Onyinye Udeh (Nee Ogbonna) is a prolific writer and holds a B.Sc. in Communication from the Enugu State University of Science and Technology, Nigeria.

Her love and passion for writing has been translated into a motion picture titled; "Nne *(The Jewel of Ukelu Kingdom)*".

"Love without Flower" is her first novel to be published amongst many others to come.

She grew up in Nigeria. She is happily married to Mr. Edwin Udeh and is blessed with two beautiful children.

She currently resides in the US with her Family.

Love without Flower